You're Mine, Walker and All

Written by Kristina M. Parker

Illustrated by Chad J. Rabideau

Good luck telling your own Story.

[signature: Kristina M. Parker]

Dedication

To my KC, for your
inspiration and
encouragement to be the
best mommy I can.

Acknowledgments

I wish to thank Chad J. Rabideau for his wonderful illustrations. To see more of Chad's artwork, visit Chad Rabideau-artist on Facebook. I also want to thank Joy A. Demarse, Ph.D. for her skills as an editor and her support and friendship. I am so grateful for my husband Michael's unwavering belief in our little family.

KC stayed with Mommy and was patient as they traveled up and down each aisle shopping, carefully choosing items. It seemed as if they had looked at millions of school supplies in one hundred aisles. They picked out new pencils, crayons, erasers, glue, and a backpack.

As Mommy's shopping bag filled, KC wished Mommy could push a shopping cart, or that she had brought a friend along to push a cart. They passed by a little boy sitting in a cart, and KC thought, "I am getting older and bigger but I still love riding."

KC imagined himself as a race car driver zipping around the racetrack of aisles, or as a rodeo cowboy waiting for the cart to turn wild, weaving at any moment. He was ready to be done shopping and waiting for Mommy. KC sighed loudly.

"We're almost done, Buddy."

KC knew Mommy was encouraging him but he was tired of shopping and he was bored.

KC felt as if he had been walking for hours around the store.   He wondered why his mommy needed to walk with her walker.

"Mommy, I want to ride in a cart. Can't you get one so I can ride like the other kids?"

"I can't push a cart because I need to have two hands on my walker while I'm walking."

"But Mommy, can't you just hold on to the cart like that man over there?" Maybe people would stop staring at them if Mommy just grabbed a cart instead of using her big cloth shopping bag.

"KC, if I walk without my walker, I will fall down. You know that."

As they headed to the checkout, Mommy and KC passed the toy aisle and KC darted ahead, shouting excitedly.

"I'll be right back, Mommy. Can I get a toy, please?"

"Yes, if you slow down and stay with me, we can choose a toy together because you have been very patient today. Thank you for not complaining about having to walk instead of getting to ride in a shopping cart."

Once his new toy was in his hands, KC forgot all about Mommy's walker and the people staring at her as they made their way to the checkout.

The checkout lady smiled sweetly and said, "Aren't you a big helper,"
as KC took the supplies from her and headed toward the car.
"Thanks." He liked when people noticed how big and strong he was.

It was windy outside, but KC was focused on his job, carrying their bag.

"Be careful, KC, and look for cars." Mommy always reminded him to be careful crossing a parking lot, especially because she held onto her walker, and not his hand. Sometimes they played red light, green light so KC knew it was safe to cross the parking lot, "Green Light!" or if he had to stop, "Red Light!" and wait for Mommy.

He tossed the shopping bag on the backseat and climbed up into the car. As they started home, Mommy and KC usually talked about their trip, and what he wanted to do when they got home, or what they might have for dinner. But today Mommy was different.

"Do you know why I have a walker?"

All KC wanted to do was play with his new shiny orange race car. But Mommy started talking.

"I have a disability; that means that I have trouble doing certain daily activities that are simple for other people. I have to do the activities differently from others."

Not looking up from his toy, KC asked, "Is that why you walk very, very slowly and carefully when you carry my dinner plate to the table, like it's dangerous dynamite that could explode?"

"Yes, that's right," Mommy chuckled. "I have to carry things a bit more slowly because I have to focus on walking too."

"But there are many kinds of disabilities. Some people are born with a disability, but others have an accident or an illness or a problem that changes their body when they are older. Many people have disabilities that we can't see by simply looking at them. I have cerebral palsy. That means that the part of my brain that tells my body how to walk was damaged when I was born, so I had to learn to walk with the help of doctors, and a teacher called a physical therapist."

Mommy went on. "They helped me learn, but I still have a hard time moving. My muscles work a little differently, so I have to walk with a walker. Some people with cerebral palsy use wheelchairs, crutches, or canes to help them move around."

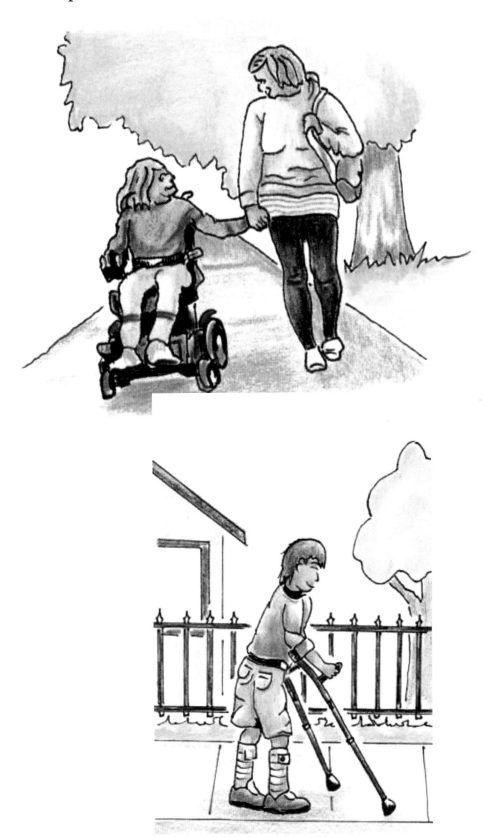

KC giggled from the backseat, looking up from his race car with a big grin. "Mommy, you're unique. I've never seen anyone else like you. There's no one else like you in the world. You're cool."

"Thank you, KC, but you didn't always think I was so cool," Mommy paused. "Do you remember going to the playground when you were little? You would cry because you wanted me to push you on the swing or use the teeter totter with you, but I couldn't use my walker and push the swing, or balance on a teeter totter."

"Remember the other day, I chose the merry-go-round instead. We compromised!" KC exclaimed.

"I know, Buddy.   Now when we go out together, we work as a team and focus on what we CAN do together. Not what we can't. Today you stayed with me in the store and even carried some of your own school supplies."

"But it wasn't always that easy for you, or me. When you were a baby I couldn't carry you around the house in my arms, so I used a front pack. Like a kangaroo joey in a pouch. But, I think you did like that, because when I walked you swayed a bit and you always fell asleep.

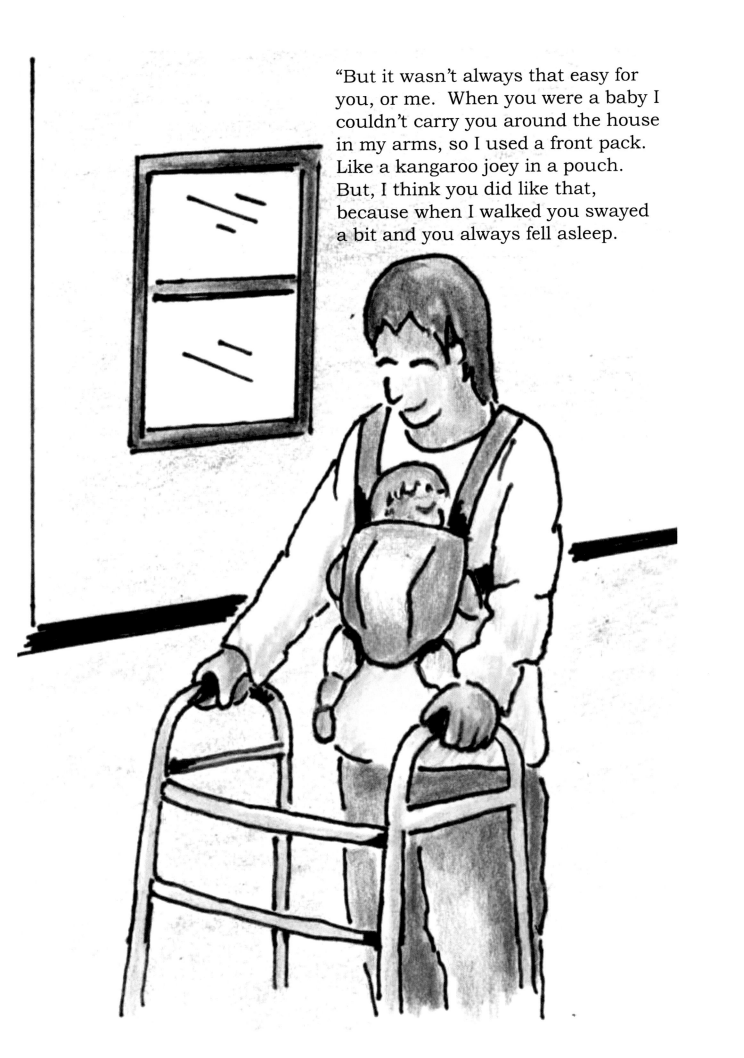

When you outgrew your front pack, I couldn't walk and push your stroller. So, Daddy and I connected your stroller to my walker for long walks. I pushed the walker and it pushed the stroller."

"Oh, like two train cars coupled up together," KC added.

"Yes, like two train cars. But you loved to walk too. I had a harness and lead made, so that we could walk safely and I could hang on to your lead and my walker."

"Did I look like that little girl with the monkey pack in the store?"
KC imagined himself in the little brown fuzzy monkey backpack.

"Sort of, but this harness was made for kids and parents with disabilities. You liked to walk inside my walker, too, especially in big crowds. Do you remember that?"

"Yes, Mommy." KC remembered going to the farmers' market, pushing Mommy's walker with her and feeling safe from the big crowds, surrounded by her metal walker.

"You're a smart little boy, and learned very young that I needed my walker to walk and you always loved to try to run away and be independent. You used to get frustrated because I was slower and could not pick you up whenever you wanted. Now that you are older, are you still annoyed waiting for me?"

"No, but sometimes I get bored, but I guess I'm used to it," KC said simply.

"I had fun a few days ago when we raced at the park. Even though you only walked fast. I loved pretending to be a grandpa turtle, running in slow motion." He beamed with pride. "I still won the race!"

"Mommy, what do you say when people look at you funny and stare?" KC asked.

"I always smile and tell them that I need to walk with a walker or I will fall down. I was born like this. I want to make sure people know they can ask questions about my disability, and learn. Just like when you ask your teacher a question in school, the answer helps you understand and learn."

Mommy continued, "Maybe if a child or grown-up asks me a question, instead of just staring, they can learn something new, and understand other people with disabilities a little better. You will meet many different people in your life, KC: try to be understanding, be kind, and remember that we are all unique."

"Mommy, when you came on my field-trip last year, my friend John stared at you. He said having you as a mom must be boring because you can't walk or play like his parents. I told him to move on. But he didn't," KC said frustratingly. "He wanted to know what we do for fun."

"What did you say?" Mom asked curiously.

"I told him I love playing soccer, fishing, and ice skating with you. When you have trouble playing sports like other parents, you have a friend come with us or have cool equipment that helps you, kind of like your walker, but a little different."

KC laughed and said, "Mommy, I wish we could find a flat mountain for you to hike, but since we can't, I bring back pictures to show you. It's almost like you were there too!"

KC and Mommy had talked all the way home. As Mommy turned off the car and reached for her walker, KC grabbed the bag of school supplies and carried it into the house. He knew he didn't always have to help his mommy, but it was easier for him to carry things, so he usually did.

After dinner and his bath, KC placed his new orange race car next to his pillow and climbed into bed. It had been a long day of shopping and he had a lot to think about after his talk with Mommy in the car. He yawned, ready for his favorite time with Mommy, bedtime.

As Mommy read to him and then tucked him in, KC thought about all Mommy had said that day.

"I love you, Buddy. Good night."

Sleepily KC replied, "Mommy, together we do everything everyone else can. You just do it in your own unique, special way. There's no one else quite like you in the whole world. You're simply mine, walker and all."

KC snuggled deeper into his bed, whispering a sleepy "Good night, Mommy."

Mommy and her walker

By KC

Made in the USA
Lexington, KY
30 October 2019